A NOTE TO PARENTS

Reading Aloud with Your Child

Research shows that reading books aloud is the single most valuable support parents can provide in helping children learn to read.

- Be a ham! The more enthusiasm you display, the more your child will enjoy the book.
- Run your finger underneath the words as you read to signal that the print carries the story.
- Leave time for examining the illustrations more closely; encourage your child to find things in the pictures.
- Invite your youngster to join in whenever there's a repeated phrase in the text.
- Link up events in the book with similar events in your child's life.
- If your child asks a question, stop and answer it. The book can be a means to learning more about your child's thoughts.

Listening to Your Child Read Aloud

The support of your attention and praise is absolutely crucial to your child's continuing efforts to learn to read.

- If your child is learning to read and asks for a word, give it immediately so that the meaning of the story is not interrupted. DO NOT ask your child to sound out the word.
- On the other hand, if your child initiates the act of sounding out, don't intervene.
- If your child is reading along and makes what is called a miscue, listen for the sense of the miscue. If the word "road" is substituted for the word "street," for instance, no meaning is lost. Don't stop the reading for a correction.
- If the miscue makes no sense (for example, "horse" for "house"), ask your child to reread the sentence because you're not sure you understand what's just been read.
- Above all else, enjoy your child's growing command of print and make sure you give lots of praise. *You are your child's first teacher — and the most important one. Praise from you is critical for further risk-taking and learning.*

— Priscilla Lynch
Ph.D., New York University
Educational Consultant

Text copyright © 1997 by Roger D. Johnston and Susan T. Johnston,
as trustees of the Johnston Family Trust.
Illustrations copyright © 1997 by Susannah Ryan.
All rights reserved. Published by Scholastic Inc.
HELLO READER! and CARTWHEEL BOOKS and associated logos
are trademarks and/or registered trademarks of Scholastic Inc.
A hardcover edition of *Sparky and Eddie: The First Day of School*
is being published simultaneously by Scholastic Press.

Library of Congress Cataloging-in-Publication Data

Johnston, Tony, 1942 –
    Sparky and Eddie : the first day of school / by Tony Johnston ; pictures by Susannah Ryan
        p.   cm.— (Hello reader! Level 3)
    "Cartwheel Books."
    Summary: Even though they are not in the same class, two young friends are glad that they decided to give school a try.
    ISBN 0-590-47979-2
    [1. First day of school — Fiction. 2. Schools — Fiction.
3. Friendship — Fiction.] I. Ryan, Susannah, ill. II. Title.
    PZ7.J6478Ss 1997
[E] — dc20   96-38192
                                                                                CIP
                                                                                AC

10 9 8 7 6 5 4 3 2 1

Printed in the U.S.A.   24
First printing, September 1997

SPARKY AND EDDIE
THE FIRST DAY OF SCHOOL

by **Tony Johnston**
pictures by **Susannah Ryan**

HELLO READER! — LEVEL 3

Cartwheel B·O·O·K·S ®

SCHOLASTIC INC.
New York Toronto London Auckland Sydney

For the *real* Sparky and Eddie,
two good friends,
two Stanford men
in grammar school again.
And for Jeffrey Dale.
(He knows why.)
— T. J.

For Claire and Phoebe
— S. R.

Sparky and Eddie lived
next door to each other.

Sparky was born on the Fourth of July.
He was named for sparklers.

Eddie was born on a plain day.
He was named for Uncle Ed.

Sparky was tall.

Eddie was short.

Sparky had freckles.

Eddie had none.

Sparky liked trees.

Eddie liked bugs.

They were so different,

they were best friends.

Sparky and Eddie played
all summer long.
They climbed trees.
They looked at bugs.
Sparky got more freckles.
Eddie got none.
Then it was time for school.

Sparky and Eddie wanted to start school.
They wanted to be in the same room, too.
Their parents took them
to school one day to see
who their teachers would be.

The room lists were up.

Sparky would have Mr. Lopez.

Eddie would have Ms. Bean.

Sparky and Eddie looked at each other.

They gasped,

"We're not in the same room!"

They felt glum.

Too glum to climb trees.

Too glum to look at bugs.

Too glum to even cry.

They stared at nothing, feeling glum.

Then Sparky said, "Let's make a deal."

"What deal?" asked Eddie.

"We're not in the same room,"
said Sparky. "So we won't
go to school."

"COOL!" shouted Eddie.

"This year we'll stay home!"

"We'll climb trees," Sparky said.

"We'll look at bugs," Eddie said.

"We'll have fun, fun, FUN!"
shouted Sparky.

Then he said, "Shake on it."

So they did.

"No switchies?" asked Eddie.

"No switchies," Sparky said.

Eddie told his mother,
"Sparky and I made a deal.
We're not in the same room,
so we won't go to school this year."
"Oh, dear," said his mother.
"Your teacher will be sad."

Sparky told his father,
"Eddie and I made a deal.
We're not in the same room,
so we won't go to school this year."
"Oh, dear," said his father.
"Your teacher will be sad."

Eddie told Sparky,

"If we don't go to school,

our teachers will be sad."

"They'll whimper," said Sparky.

"They'll whine," Eddie said.

"They'll blubber."

"They'll cry like rain."

Sparky and Eddie felt so sad about that,

they almost cried like rain.

"What can we do?" Sparky asked.

Eddie thought.

He thought.

And thought.

Then Eddie said,
"We'll give them a chance.
If we like them, we'll stay."
"If we don't, we'll go home,"
said Sparky.
"We'll climb trees.
We'll look at bugs.
We'll have fun, fun, FUN!"
"This is a switchy," said Eddie.
"That's O.K.," said Sparky.
"It's a nice switchy. Is it a deal?"
"Deal," Eddie said.
And they shook on it.

It was the first day of school.
Eddie went to his room.
Ms. Bean was waiting, smiling.

She had a rhinoceros beetle on her desk.

Eddie thought it was beautiful.

Ms. Bean let the kids look at it.

She let the kids touch it.

Some kids said, "Oooh!"

Some kids said, "Aaah!"

Eddie said, "*OOOH!*" and "*AAAH!*"

Sparky went to his room.

Mr. Lopez was waiting, smiling.

He had a bonsai on his desk.

The bonsai was short.

A dwarf, really. A dwarf tree.

Mr. Lopez let the kids look at it.

He let the kids touch it.

Some kids said, "Oooh!"

Some kids said, "Aaah!"

Sparky said, *"OOOH!"*

and *"AAAH!"*

Sparky and Eddie met
at the boys' bathroom.
"Do you like your teacher?" asked Eddie.
"Yes," said Sparky.
"He has a bonsai on his desk."

"What's that?" Eddie asked.

"A short tree."

"Short like me?"

"Shorter."

"COOL!" Eddie said.

"Do you like your teacher?"
asked Sparky.

"Yes," said Eddie.

"She has a rhinoceros beetle on her desk."

"WOW!" Sparky yelled.

"*A rhinoceros on her desk!*"

"It's a beetle," said Eddie.

Then he said,

"School is fun. I will stay.

I can be your best friend,

even if we're not in the same room."

"Me, too," said Sparky.

"Sparky?" asked Eddie.
"Could I see your teacher's bonsai?
I want to see something
shorter than I am."

"Sure," said Sparky.

"Could I see your teacher's rhinoceros?
I want to see a rhinoceros on a desk."

"It's a *beetle*, Sparky."

"I know," said Sparky.

"And I want to see it."

Eddie said, "O.K.
We'll see it after school."

"O.K.," said Sparky.

"Let's make a deal.
 Beetles and bonsai after school."

"Cool," said Eddie.

"But this time, no switchies."

Then they shook on it.